Imagine That!

ELIZABETH BEST

Illustrated by Paul Harrison

sundance
A Haights Cross Communications Company

The Story Characters

Pete
has a house with
a secret tunnel.

Joe
is Pete's new friend.

Pete's mom
goes out for awhile.

The Story Setting

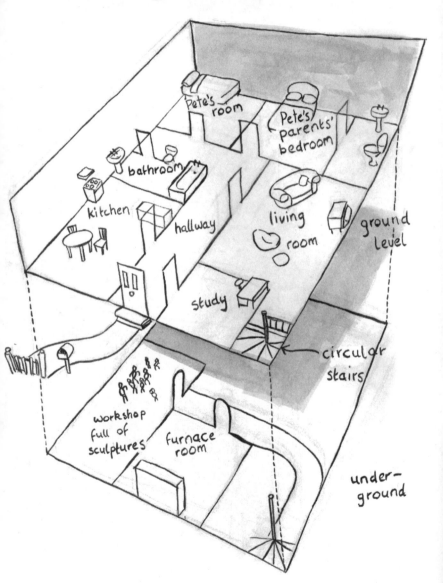

Pete's room

Pete's parents' bedroom

bathroom

kitchen

hallway

living room

ground level

study

circular stairs

workshop full of sculptures

furnace room

under- ground

TABLE OF CONTENTS

CHAPTER 1

Pete's Secret Tunnel

"Do you want to see under my house?" said Pete to his new friend.

"Yes," said Joe, "but why?"

"Everyone wants to see under my house. It's really spooky. You don't have to go outside first. You just go down the circular stairs. You walk down to the bottom, and there's this tunnel and . . ."

"Let's go then," said Joe.

"Um . . . we can't go yet," said Pete.

"Why not?"

"We'll just wait until Mom goes out. She's going across the street to see Mrs. Phillips," Pete said, in a whisper.

"Why do we have to wait?" asked Joe.

"Mom doesn't like me going down there anymore," said Pete quietly.

"Why not?" Joe asked.

"You know how I want to be rich when I grow up?" said Pete.

"Yes."

"Well, I was making my friends pay 50 cents to go under the house. Only 50 cents. That's not much."

Pete went on. "Mom says I can't do it anymore. She doesn't care that she is keeping me poor. She doesn't care about that at all!"

"Are you going to make me pay?" asked Joe.

"I told you, I'm not supposed to," Pete said, with a frown.

"Good," said Joe.

Then Pete smiled, "But you can make a donation. You know how a lot of people make donations to good causes? Well, I think that my future is a good cause."

Pete's mom called, "Pete, I'm just going across the street to see Mrs. Phillips."

"Bye, Mom," said Pete.

CHAPTER 2

The Dark Tunnel

The door slammed.

"Now!" said Pete.

They crossed the hall to the circular stairway. Down they both went.

The tunnel was at the bottom of the stairs. The light was dim at first, but soon it became pitch-black. Joe sucked in his breath. He'd always been a little scared of the dark.

15

"Don't put your hands on the walls," Pete said. "You might get bitten."

"Nothing lives down here," Joe said, his voice shaking a little. "It's too dark."

"What about spiders? They live in the dark," said Pete.

Joe took his hands off the wall. Quickly.

The narrow tunnel went around a corner. Joe's head scraped along some bricks.

"I don't know where I'm going. I need to touch the walls," said Joe.

"Follow me," said Pete. "I know the way. Just listen to my footsteps."

Then something trailed across Joe's face. "Hey, stop!" he screamed. "Something is on my face."

"Cobwebs," said Pete. "Don't worry about them."

Joe pulled at them. He tried to get them off, but they were sticky.

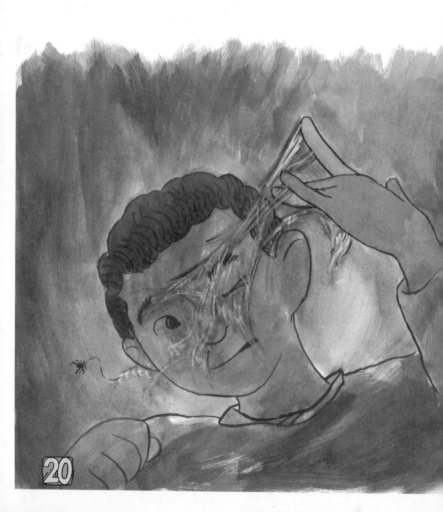

"Look out," said Pete. Then he added, "Watch your step here."

It was too late. Joe stepped on to some empty cans. They rolled under his feet, and he rolled with them. He landed in the dirt, on his hands and knees.

Spiders or no spiders, Joe was going to hold onto the walls now.

As they walked by an opening to a room, Pete said, "We'd better hurry past here."

Joe tried to hurry. He wanted to ask why, but he was out of breath.

BOOM! There was a loud noise. The sound bounced off the walls of the room and into the tunnel. Joe jumped, and his heart pounded.

"See what I mean?" said Pete.

"What was that?" Joe asked, trying to sound calm.

"I'm not sure," said Pete, in a strange voice. "There's an old furnace in that room. Maybe it makes that noise when it starts up."

Now the tunnel opened out into a
large room. The room was dimly lit.
Joe saw a man in the corner. His
heart leaped in shock. His throat
closed. He couldn't speak.

Joe stood still. Then he started to see more people. They were all around him. The room was full of people.

27

CHAPTER 3

Who Are These People?

All of the people stood very still. Their stillness was scary. There was something very strange about them.

"These are Dad's sculptures," said Pete.
"He used to be a sculptor, but he gave
it up."

Suddenly the room was full of light,
and Pete was laughing.

29

"There are lights all of the way," Pete said. "But I think it's more fun to come down here in the dark, don't you? Were you scared?" he asked.

Joe stared at the sculptures. His heart was still in his throat, and his hands were all wet. He tried to smile.

Then they heard footsteps above them.

"Uh-oh!" said Pete. "Mom's back. Now I'm in trouble." He started walking back along the tunnel.

"I'll put on the lights now. Can you be very quiet so she doesn't know we're down here? OK? We'll try to sneak up the stairs without her knowing," Pete whispered.

Joe nodded his head.

CHAPTER 4

Heavy Footsteps

They moved slowly and carefully. Heavy footsteps thumped above them.

Joe whispered, "Does your mom wear heavy boots?"

"No . . . why?" asked Pete.

"Listen to the footsteps."

"You're right!" said Pete. He stopped walking. "That's not Mom!"

"Is it your dad?" asked Joe.

"Dad won't be home for ages," Pete said. "It must be a burglar. Listen!"

They both listened. The footsteps were moving from one end of the house to the other.

"He'll wreck the place," Pete whispered. "That's Mom's bedroom he's in now. He must be stealing all of her jewelry."

"Does your mom have a lot of jewelry?" asked Joe.

"Not much, no. Now she'll have nothing."

"We have to do something!" said Joe.
"I think that we should call the
police." His heart started thumping
again. He was really scared now.

"That's it, Joe. Good idea! We'll sneak into the kitchen and call the police."

They could still hear the footsteps
overhead.

"We'll wait until he goes to the other
end of the house," said Pete.

"OK."

The sound of the footsteps faded. Pete
and Joe crept up the stairs.

They darted across the hall and into the kitchen. The telephone was in the corner.

Pete lifted the telephone. Then, with a
shock, they heard Pete's mom.

"I'm home, Pete!" she called.

Before they could speak, she walked
through the house toward her
bedroom.

"Quick, stop her!" cried Joe, grabbing Pete's arm. "The burglar will see her."

"He'll probably hide when he hears her coming," said Pete.

CHAPTER 5

Saving Pete's Mom

"What if he doesn't? What if he hurts her?" Joe was shaking like a leaf. "Do something," he hissed at Pete.

"If you knew Mom like I know Mom, you wouldn't worry," said Pete. "My mom's a match for any burglar."

"You're a coward!" said Joe, in Pete's ear. "You don't care if your own mother gets hurt."

There was the sound of a man's voice.

"Well, if you won't go help her, I will!" Joe said. He raced down the hall to the bedroom. The burglar and Pete's mom were in the bedroom.

Joe jumped. He landed with all of his force on the man's back.

"Leave her alone!" Joe shouted.

"What the . . . ?" the man said,
swinging around. He sent Joe
spinning to the floor.

"It's all right, Joe," said Pete's mom. "This is Pete's dad. He's not hurting me. We were just hugging."

Joe jumped up and stood looking at them. Then he turned and ran out of the room.

"You knew it was your dad all of the time, didn't you?" Joe snarled at Pete.

Pete nodded. "I'm going to make movies when I grow up," he said. "So I need to know how to make scary things happen."

"I'm going home," said Joe angrily.

As Joe headed toward the door, Pete said, "Don't be mad at me. To make scary movies, I have to do things to see how people behave when they're frightened. But I think I went too far this time."

Then Pete remembered that Joe liked to write. "You're a great writer, Joe," he called out. "If you stay, we could write a scary movie. Together, we could make exciting things happen!"

Joe stopped and thought for a moment. Then he came back.

"Hey, I have an idea. You could make someone come down from outer space," said Joe. "That would be better than an old burglar!"

"How about if I had things coming up out of the ground? Monsters and things," said Pete. "That would be really creepy."

"Wait! I've got another idea!" cried Joe. "What about a mad doctor? Every time you go to the doctor, he takes some part out of you. First it's an eye. Then it's a kidney or something, and he won't give it back!"

"No! No way! That's too scary," said Pete. "That scares me to death!"

GLOSSARY

burglar
a thief who breaks
in to steal things

circular
going around in a circle

darted
ran quickly

donation
money given to
help someone else

pitch-black
very, very, very dark

sculptor
someone who carves
sculptures

sculptures
solid artistic shapes
made by carving

snarled
yelled at

Talking with the Author and the Illustrator

Elizabeth Best (author)

If you could go anywhere, where would it be?
 To the bottom of my garden, where the fairies live.

Why is the sky blue?
 Because they ran out of pink.

What are three things that you can't live without?
 My children, my books, and music.

Paul Harrison (illustrator)

Who is your favorite cartoon character?
 Calvin, because he always finds the trapdoor to
 his imagination.

Why is the sky blue?
 So it is always easy to recognize.

What are three things that you can't live without?
 Sleep, fun, and someone to do things with.

Copyright © 2002 Sundance Publishing

Published by Sundance Publishing
P.O. Box 1326, 234 Taylor Street, Littleton, MA 01460
800-343-8204

Copyright © text Elizabeth Best
Copyright © illustrations Paul Harrison

First published 1999 as Sparklers by
Blake Education, Locked Bag 2022, Glebe 2037, Australia
Exclusive United States Distribution: Sundance Publishing

ISBN 0-7608-8139-5

Printed in Canada